THE STORY
OF THE
INDIAN NATIONAL FLAG

THE STORY
OF THE
INDIAN NATIONAL FLAG
TIRANGA

GHANTASALA GOPIKRISHNA

DEDICATION

This book is in dedication to all the Indians, irrespective of their caste, religion, or region. India means not just a piece of land but a diverse and vibrant tapestry of cultures, traditions, and beliefs that make up its rich heritage.

It is a celebration of unity in diversity and the collective spirit that binds all Indians together.

May this book inspire us to continue honoring our heritage and working towards a brighter future for India.

Let the colors of the flag symbolize unity, courage, and hope as we strive to make a difference in our country.

The Author

Table of Contents

DEDICATION

PREFACE

ACKNOWLEDGEMENTS

INTRODUCTION

CHAPTER ONE

PINGALI VENKAIAH

Glimpses of Pingali Venkaiah life

CHAPTER TWO

BOER WAR

CHAPTER THREE

CONGRESS & the FLAG

Chapter FOUR

The Flag Resolution 1947

CHAPTER FIVE

THE ORIGINS OF THE FLAG

CHAPTER SIX

THE FLAGS OF OTHER NATIONS

CHAPTER SEVEN

THE TYABJI FAMILY

ABOUT THE AUTHOR

PREFACE

It has been seventy-eight years since India got independence from the British. The selfless persons who sought independence for India's future generations are no more. May be a few persons, who were kids at that time, and who are fortunate to live a hundred + years might be alive to tell us the stories of the struggle for India's independence.

The history of India is not known to the present generations. Our present generations are not aware of the national symbols. The artificial intelligence technology did not write the national anthem, or it did not design the national flag.

There was a lot of struggle, pain, and sacrifice involved in achieving independence. It is important for the youth of today to learn about the rich history and heritage of their country in order to appreciate the sacrifices made by their ancestors to make us live happily today with freedom of speech and expression.

By understanding the struggles of the past, the youth can also be inspired to contribute positively towards the future of their nation. Learning about the sacrifices made during India's fight for independence can instill a sense of pride and responsibility in the younger generation.

The purpose of compiling this book is to give clarity to the present and future generations about the Indian national flag and who designed it in a simple language.

The author's intention is to ensure that the true history and contributions of individuals are accurately documented and acknowledged. By shedding light on some of the discrepancies, the author hopes to uphold the integrity of historical records for future generations without any bias and with due respect to all.

The Author

Jallianwala Bagh Massacre

जलियाँवाला बाग
ਜਲ੍ਹਿਆਂਵਾਲਾ ਬਾਗ
JALLIANWALA BAGH

ACKNOWLEDGEMENTS

The author respects the copyrights and tenders his apology for any infringement of copyrights to all the photographers, publishers, websites, and individuals for using some photos and data without prior permission.

The author owns most of the photos used in this book.

The author requests the copy right owners of a few photos to pardon and hopes that they accept the apologies.

The book is a compilation and was written as per the experience and perception of the author, with due respect to everyone mentioned in this book, as the grandson of Pingali Venkaiah, the architect of the Indian national flag.

Our wholehearted gratitude to the Wanderers Bulleteers, Hyderabad, for celebrating Pingali Venkaiah's birthday since 2015.

Our special thanks to Mr. G. Vasu Deva Nandana Narasimham, author of Pingali Venkaiah's biography.

This book is only for factual information and not to harm or defame any individual or organization, knowingly or unknowingly. The author hopes that readers will appreciate the effort put into compiling this information and find it informative and enlightening.

Author

INTRODUCTION

Did you know that the idea of an Indian national flag triggered in South Africa?

Did you know why Mahatma Gandhi asked Pingali Venkaiah to make a design for the Congress or national flag in 1921?

Did you know who Pingali Venkaiah is?

There were thousands of great leaders in the Congress at that time. But he chose Pingali Venkaiah for a specific reason. Pingali Venkaiah was the first person to conceptualize having a flag for the nation or the Congress, and Mahatma Gandhi chose him because of this, along with his role as a freedom fighter.

His design for the flag needed to symbolize unity and represent the diversity of India's people, which Venkaiah achieved with his unique design.

Pingali Venkaiah met Gandhiji for the first time when he was a young soldier fighting the Boers in South Africa, and Gandhiji served the wounded soldiers through his sevadal under the Red Cross society in South Africa.

This encounter left a lasting impression on Venkaiah, leading to their collaboration on the design of the Indian national flag. Venkaiah's flag design was eventually adopted as the official flag of India on July 22, 1947.

The reasons for the ambiguity and misunderstanding in some could be due to the following reasons:

1. The author of "The History of Congress," Bogaraju Pattabhi Seetha Ramaiah, had forgotten to write about the story of the flag, which was the important trigger in the struggle for independence.

2. Mr. Trevor Royale mentioned in his book "The Last Days of the Raj." that **Mrs. Suraya Tyabji designed the flag for the prime minister's car on Independence Day.**

3. Pandit Jawaharlal Nehru, the first Prime Minister of India, did not mention either Pingali Venkaiah or Suraya, who replaced the charkha with the Ashok chakra, in his speech on the occasion of accepting the resolution of the flag in the parliament (constituent assembly).

However, he mentioned that many freedom fighters died to protect the flag in the war of independence in the last two decades, before independence.

Is this not evidence indicating that the flag designed by Pingali Venkaiah in 1921 and accepted by Gandhiji is modified and adopted as the national flag?

Mahatma Gandhi himself acknowledged that Pingali Venkaiah designed the flag in his article in "Young India." on April 13, 1921.

Young India.

Ahmedabad, Wednesday, 13th, April, 1921.

THE NATIONAL FLAG.

(By M. K. Gandhi)

A flag is a necessity for all nations. Millions have died for it. It is no doubt a kind of idolatry which it would be a sin to destroy. For a flag represents an ideal. The unfurling of the Union Jack evokes in the English breast, sentiments whose strength it is difficult to measure. The Stars and Stripes mean a world to the Americans. The Star and the Crescent will call forth the best bravery in Islam.

It will be necessary for us Indians—Hindus, Mahomedans, Christians, Jews, Parsis, and all others to whom India is their home—to recognise a common flag to live and to die for.

Mr. P. Venkayya of the National College Masulipatam has for some years placed before the public a suggestive booklet describing the flags of the other nations and offering designs for an Indian National Flag. But, whilst I have always admired the persistent zeal with which Mr. Venkayya has prosecuted the cause of a national flag at every session of the Congress for the past four years, he was never able to enthuse me; and in his designs I saw nothing to stir the nation to its depths. It was reserved for a Punjabee to make a suggestion that at once arrested attention. It was Lala Hansraj of Jullunder who, in discussing the possibilities of the spinning wheel, suggested that it should find a place on our Swaraj Flag. I could not help admiring the originality of the suggestion. At Bezwada I asked Mr. Venkayya to give me a design containing a spinning wheel on a red (Hindu colour) and green (Muslim colour) background. His enthusiastic spirit enabled me to possess a flag in three hours.

CHAPTER ONE

PINGALI VENKAIAH

In his last days at Vijayawada

Pingali Venkaiah was born on August 2, 1878, in Peddakallepalli (not Batlapenumarru, as everyone claims) in the Krishna district of Andhra Pradesh to Hanumantha Rayudu and Venkata Ratnam.

He was born in the house of his maternal grandfather, Adavi Venkatachalapathi, and grandmother, Sitamma, in Pedakallepalli.

Pedakallepalli school where Pingali studied

Entry page in the School Admission Register

(The photos show the school he studied in Pedakallepalli and the school register showing Pingali Venkaiah's name and roll no: 65, and the guardian as Hanumanth Rayudu, his father)

The author is not aware of how and why people quote Batlapenumarru as his birthplace. It is important to clarify the correct birthplace of Pingali Venkaiah to honor his true origins and legacy.

The misinformation surrounding his birthplace may have stemmed from confusion or a lack of accurate historical records with the government.

At the age of 19, Venkaiah had enrolled in the British Indian Army and was deployed to South Africa during the Second Boer War (1899–1902).

During the war, when the soldiers had to salute the Union Jack, the national flag of Britain, Venkaiah realized the need for having a flag for Indians.

In fact, he got the idea in his school days and it became strong in the Boer War. He could not do anything in the war except salute, as there is a possibility of court martial.

When Venkaiah attended the AICC session in 1906 in Calcutta, he was inspired to design a flag for the Indian National Congress, as he opposed the idea of unfurling the British flag at Congress meetings.

All the national leaders who attended the meeting know Pingali Venkaiah's zeal, and there was no objection to entrusting the job of designing the flag to Venkaiah.

His reputation for creativity and dedication preceded him, making him the obvious choice for such an important task. The unanimous decision to appoint him speaks volumes about the trust and respect he commands among his peers.

Gandhiji selected a flag with red and green colors from the twenty-five designs shown by Venkaiah, to which Lala Hans Raj and Gandhiji later added a spinning wheel (Charkha) and a white stripe, respectively.

Pingali Venkaiah was a multi-talented person holding masters in geology and agriculture. He was also a multilingual and eloquent speaker in many languages.

He never participated in politics after India attained independence. He lived a simple life and did not ever disclose that he designed the Indian national flag.

He lost his younger son and faced difficult times in his last days. He never asked for help.

Knowing his poverty, Congress leaders like Siris Raju, Tenneti Chalapathi Rao, Ayyadevara Kaleswar Rao, etc. arranged the bare necessities in his home without his knowledge, by convincing his wife.

Felicitation in rice miller's association hall before his death

Despite facing hardships in his final days, Pingali Venkaiah remained humble and never sought assistance from others. His contribution to designing the Indian national flag remained unknown to many until after his passing away.

Glimpses of Pingali Venkaiah life

·   Pingali Venkaiah was born on August 2, 1878, in Peddakallepalli (not Batlapenumarru, as everyone claims) in the Krishna district of Andhra Pradesh.

·   Pingali Venkaiah's lineage is from Pingali Moropant, Jhansi Lakshmi bhai, and also Pingali Madanna, who worked as commander in chief of army in Golconda fort for Hyderabad ruler.

·   At the age of 19 years, he fought the Boer War even though he did not like it. (Went to war as his duty)

·   Pingali Venkaiah studied political science and economics in Ceylon (Srilanka) and passed senior Cambridge along with agricultural science. His innovative ideas in hybrid cotton brought him the fame "Cotton Venkaiah.".

·   He has masters in geology and authored a book on diamonds, "Diamond Lore," so he was called "Diamond Venkaiah.".

·   He studied Japanese language from Professor Goethe in DAV College Lahore, which was run by Sri Lala Hansraj. He was fluent in English, Hindi, Urdu, and Sanskrit.

·   He was disturbed to salute Union Jack in a 1906 Congress meeting, and the idea of an Indian flag generated in his brain.

· He started collecting the information on various flags across the globe and authored a book on flags.

· Started convincing Congress leaders with his eloquent speeches.

· On March 31, 1921, Gandhiji asked him to bring a design. He designed the flag within 3 hours and handed over the design in Victoria Museum (now Bapu Museum) on 31-03-1921.

· He worked in various capacities as Railway guard, agriculturist and geologist for livelihood.

· He has two sons and only one daughter.

· Pingali Venkaiah died on July 4,1963 in Vijayawada

Eldest son:

1. Pingali Parasurammaiah—geologist/Indian express correspondent—Damayanthi. He has three daughters.

The following photo is used by many media channels and newspapers, claiming it as Pingali Venkaiah, which is not right.

2. Seethamahalakshmi-Housewife-Ghantasala Vugra Narasimham-Banker. She lived 100 years.

She has three sons and three daughters.

M.Chaya Devi-w/o.Late. MS. Rama Rao, eldest daughter—She has four sons and one daughter

Late. GDN. Narasimham Late. G. Rama Devi, eldest son—He had one daughter and one son

GVN Narasimham G. Satya Lakshmi, younger son—He has two sons

G. Gopikrishna G. Suneetha, the youngest son-He has only one daughter

S. Radha w/o. S. Atchytha Rao, younger daughter—She has two daughters

K. Sujatha w/o. KSK.Dhanvantari, youngest daughter—She has two daughters.

3. Pingali Chalapathi Rao-Milatary Service, Mrs.
Janaki.

Pingali Chalapathi Rao and his wife Janaki

He has one son and one daughter.

Late. Pingali Dasaratha Ram, editor of Encounter magazine,
He married Suseela and has one daughter and two sons.

Dasratha Ram and his wife Suseela

Pingali Dasaratha Ram with his children

Late.Girija w/o. Subrahmanyam -She has one daughter and one son.

Former CM OF AP felicitating the only daughter of Pingali Venkaiah in 2021

CHAPTER TWO

BOER WAR

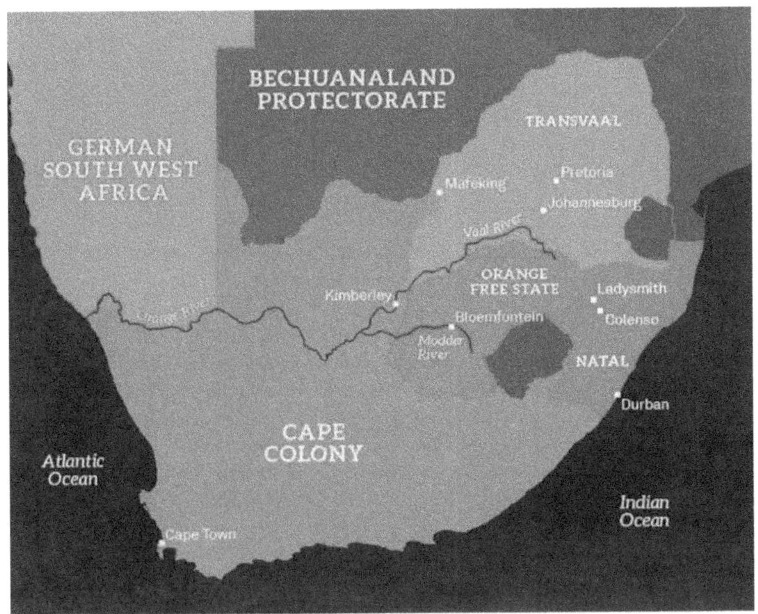

The Second Boer War, 'Second Freedom War',

(11 October 1899–31 May 1902), also known as the Boer War, Transvaal War, Anglo-Boer War, or South African War, was a conflict fought between the British Empire and the two Boer republics (the South African Republic and Orange Free State) over the Empire's influence in South Africa.

The Witwatersrand Gold Rush caused a large influx of "foreigners" to the South African Republic, mostly British from the Cape Colony (now Cape of Good Hope).

They were not permitted to vote and were regarded as "unwelcome visitors," so they protested to the British authorities in the Cape. Negotiations failed at the Bloemfontein conference in June 1899.

The conflict broke out in October when Boer irregulars and militias attacked British colonial settlements. The Boers placed Ladysmith, Kimberley, and Mafeking under siege and won victories at Colenso, Magerfontein and Stormberg. Increased numbers of the British Army soldiers were brought to Southern Africa and mounted unsuccessful attacks against the Boers.

However, British fortunes changed when their commanding officer, General Ravers Buller, was replaced by Lord Roberts and Lord Kitchener, who relieved the besieged cities and invaded the Boer republics in early 1900 at the head of a 180,000-strong expeditionary force.

The Boers, aware they were unable to resist such a large force, refrained from fighting pitched battles, allowing the British to occupy both republics and their capitals, Pretoria and Bloemfontein. Boer politicians, including President of the South African Republic Paul Kruger, either fled or went into hiding; the British Empire officially annexed the two republics in 1900.

In Britain, the Conservative ministry led by Lord Salisbury attempted to capitalize on British military successes by calling an early general election, dubbed by contemporary observers as a "Khaki election." However, Boer fighters took to the hills and launched a guerrilla campaign, becoming known as bittereinders. Boer guerrillas used hit-and-run attacks and ambushes against the British for two years.

The guerrilla campaign proved difficult for the British to defeat, due to unfamiliarity with guerrilla tactics and extensive support for the guerrillas among civilians.

In response to failures to defeat the guerrillas, British high command ordered scorched earth policies as part of a large scale and multi-pronged counter surgency campaign; a network of nets, blockhouses, strongpoints and barbed wire fences was constructed, virtually partitioning the occupied republics.

Over 100,000 Boer civilians, mostly women and children, were forcibly relocated into concentration camps, where 26,000 died, mostly by starvation and disease.

Black Africans were interned in concentration camps to prevent them from supplying the Boers; 20,000 died. British mounted infantry was deployed to track down guerrillas, leading to small-scale skirmishes.

Few combatants on either side were killed in action, with most casualties dying from disease. Kitchener offered generous terms of surrender to remaining Boer leaders to end the conflict.

Eager to ensure fellow Boers were released from the camps, most Boer commanders accepted the British terms in the Treaty of Vereeniging, surrendering in May 1902.

The former republics were transformed into the British colonies of the Transvaal and Orange River, and in 1910 they were merged with the Natal and Cape Colonies to form the Union of South Africa, a self-governing dominion within the British Empire.

British expeditionary efforts were aided significantly by colonial forces from the Cape Colony, the Natal, Rhodesia, and many volunteers from the British Empire worldwide, particularly Australia, Canada, India, and New Zealand.

Black African recruits contributed increasingly to the British war effort. International public opinion was sympathetic to the Boers and hostile to the British. Even within the UK, there existed significant opposition to the war.

As a result, the Boer cause attracted thousands of volunteers from neutral countries, including the German Empire, the United States, Russia, and even some parts of the British Empire, such as Australia and Ireland.

Some consider the war the beginning of questioning the British Empire's veneer of impenetrable global dominance, due to the war's surprising duration and the unforeseen losses suffered by the British. A trail for British war crimes committed during the war, including the killings of civilians and prisoners, was opened in January 1901.

Troops on behalf of the British

The British India decided to send troops from India to participate in the Boer War. Pingali Venkaiah, who joined the army as a 19-year-old boy, was also sent to the war. He was disturbed and mentally agitated to salute the then official flag of Great Britain, " The Union Jack.

Incidentally, he met Mohan Das Karam Chand Gandhi, who was in South Africa as a lawyer and was already doing the service through his volunteer organization "Sevadal" to the wounded soldiers on behalf of the Red Cross Society.

Pingali Venkaiah returned to India after the war and was felicitated by the government with a medal.

CHAPTER THREE

CONGRESS & the FLAG

Retired British Indian Civil Service (ICS) officer Allan Octavian Hume founded the Indian National Congress to form a platform for civil and political dialogue among educated Indians.

The East India Company transferred the control of India to the British Empire after the Indian rebellion of 1857.

British-controlled India, known as the British Raj, worked to support and justify its governance of India with the aid of English-educated Indians, who tended to be more familiar with and friendly to British culture and political thinking.

On December 28, 1885, the Indian National Congress was founded at Gokuldas Tejpal Sanskrit College in Bombay, with 72 delegates in attendance

The Prominent delegates included Dadabhai Naoroji, Surendra Nath Benerjee, **Badruddin Tyabji,** Pherozshah Mehta, W.C. Benerjee, S. Ramaswami Mudaliar, S. Subrahmanya Iyer, and Romesh Chunder Dutt.

Hume assumed office as the General Secretary, and Womesh Chunder Banerjee of Calcutta was elected president.

Congressmen saw themselves as loyalists but wanted an active role in governing their own country, albeit as part of the Empire.

The first national flag was designed by Sister Nivedita in 1904. She designed the flag with dual colors of yellow and red with a symbol of Vajra, a weapon of Lord Indra. The red and yellow colors stood for freedom and victory, whereas the Vajra symbolized strength.

Dadabhai Naoroji was considered the eldest Indian statesman by many. Naoroji went as far as contesting, successfully, an election to the British House of Commons, becoming its first

Indian member. That he was aided in his campaign by young, aspiring Indian student activists like Muhammad Ali Jinnah.

Bal Gangadhar Tilak was among the first Indian nationalists to embrace **Swaraj** as the destiny of the nation. Tilak deeply opposed the British colonial education system in India, which he thought ignored and defamed India's culture, history, and values, defying and disgracing the Indian culture.

The moderates, led by Gopala Krishna Gokhale, Pherozeshah Mehta, and Dadabhai Naoroji, held firm to calls for negotiations and political dialogue.

Gokhale criticized Tilak for encouraging acts of violence and disorder. The Congress of 1906 did not have public membership, and thus Tilak and his supporters were forced to leave the party.

Venkaiah worked on potential designs that could be used as flags for the newly coined Swaraj movement to signify independence. There were over 25 drafts of the flags with different significance and relations with Indian culture, heritage, and history.

Pingali Venkaiah attended the Congress meeting in 1906 held in Calcutta for the first time to propagate the necessity of a national flag for India, when all the delegates saluted the Union Jack, Pingali Venkaiah was upset.

He addressed the delegates and spoke spontaneously. The leaders, convinced by his eloquent speech, nominated him to the "decision-making council" of the Congress.

The flag of Swaraj was unfurled in Calcutta's session of the Indian National Congress in 1906 by Dada Bhai Naoroji.

Flag unfurled by Dada Bhai Naroji in 1906

Bikaji Cama unfurled one of the earliest versions of the flag of independent India on August 22, 1907, and she was the first person to hoist an Indian flag in a foreign nation at the International Socialist Conference at Stuttgart.

Bhikaiji Cama was born in Bombay (now Mumbai) in a large, affluent Parsi Zoroastrian family.

Her parents, Sorabji Framji Patel and Jaijibai Sorabji Patel, were well known in the city, where her father Sorabji—a lawyer by training and a merchant by profession—was an influential member of the Parsi community.

The divided Congress re-united in the pivotal Lucknow session of 1916 with the efforts of Bal Gangadhar Tilak and Muhammad Ali Jinnah.

In 1916, Pingali Venkaiah published a book titled *Bharatha Desaniki Oka Jatiya Patakam* (transl. A National Flag for India) with 30 potential designs for a flag.

From 1918 to 1921, he proposed various ideas to the Congress leadership while also working as a lecturer in National college, Machilipatnam.

Tilak had considerably moderated his views and now favored political dialogue with the British.

He, along with the young Muhammad Ali Jinnah and Mrs. Annie Besant, launched the Home Rule Movement to put forth Indian demands for *Home Rule*—Indian participation in the affairs of their own country—a precursor to *Swaraj*.

Annie Besant was born on October 1, 1847.She was a British socialist, women's rights activist and Home Rule activist, educationist, and campaigner for Indian nationalism. She was an ardent supporter of both Irish and Indian self-rule. She became the first female president of the Indian National Congress in 1917.

The All India Home Rule League was formed to demand dominion status within the Empire.

But another Indian man with another way was destined to lead the Congress and the Indian struggle. Mohandas Gandhi was a lawyer who successfully led the struggle of Indians in South Africa against South African discriminatory laws.

Returning to India in 1915, Gandhi looked to Indian culture and history and the values and lifestyle of its people to empower a new revolution. With the concepts of nonviolence and civil disobedience, he coined the term Satyagraha.

Mohandas Karamchand Gandhi, who later on became more popular as Mahatma Gandhi, had success in defeating the British in Champaran.

Mahatma Gandhi led the Champaran Satyagraha, a peasant uprising in the Champaran district of Bihar.

Champaran Satyagraha

The farmers in the region revolted against the British power against the imposed indigo cultivation between 1914 and 1916.

The Kheda Satyagraha of 1918 was a satyagraha movement in the Kheda district of Gujarat in India organized by Mahatma Gandhi during the period of the British Raj.

Kheda Satyagraha

It was a major revolt in the Indian independence movement.
It was the second Satyagraha movement, which was launched
7 days after the Ahmedabad mill strike, giving India its first
victory in the struggle for freedom.

Then the Indian National Congress supported that movement;
Indians gained confidence in the workings of that
organization and believed that the British could be thwarted
through it, and millions of young people from across the
country flooded into Congress membership.

The Vijayawada meeting of the AICC, held in 1921, marked
a crucial turning point in the struggle for Indian
independence as it was here that Mahatma Gandhi's
leadership of the national struggle was accepted by the
political leaders.

Among the crucial resolutions passed at this session included
fundraising for the Tilak Swaraj Fund, a mass enrollment

program for the Congress, and extensive promotion of the Charkha.

In this meeting Gandhiji asked Pingali Venkaiah to present his famous design for the national flag from a set of 30 designs, he made.

The Congress session of 1921 was held in Bezwada (now Vijayawada) in an open ground (now Gandhinagar), and the flag, which was designed in just three hours with the help of a colleague, Eeranki Venkata Sastry, an artist, was submitted to Gandhi Ji at the Victoria Jubilee Museum (now renamed as Bapu Museum). Gandhiji selected a flag with red and green.

In April 1921, Mahatma Gandhi wrote in his journal Young India about the need for an Indian flag, proposing a flag with the charkha, or spinning wheel, at the center.

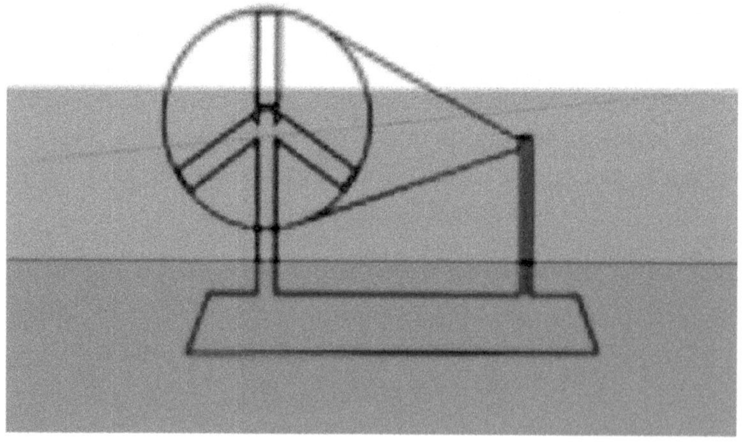

Lala Hansraj proposed the idea of a spinning wheel as a symbol for the Indian national movement. Gandhi then asked Pingali Venkayya to create a flag with a red, green and white banner, bearing a spinning wheel as its emblem.

Initially the red color represented Hindus, while the green signified Muslims. Gandhi wanted the flag to be presented at the Congress session of 1921 but could not adopt it due to lack of time.

Gandhi later wrote that the delay was fortuitous since it allowed him to realize that other religions were not represented; he then added white to the banner colors to represent all the other religions.

Finally, owing to the religious-political sensibilities, in 1929, Gandhi moved towards a more secular interpretation of the flag colors, stating that red stood for the sacrifices of the people, white for purity, and green for hope.

Pandit Motilal Nehru unfurled the flag for the first time in India at the town hall of Jubbalpore in 1922, as stated in Seth Govind Das's speech on the flag adoption resolution in the constituent assembly (parliament).

On 13 April 1923, local Congress volunteers held a procession in Nagpur to commemorate the Jallianwala Bagh massacre. The *Swaraj* flag with spinning wheel, designed by Pingali Venkaiah, was hoisted.

This event resulted in a confrontation between the Congressmen and the police, after which five people were imprisoned. Over 100 other protesters continued the flag procession after a meeting.

Subsequently, on the first of May, Jamnal Bajaj, the secretary of the Nagpur Congress Committee, started the Flag Satyagraha, gaining national attention and marking a significant point in the flag movement.

The satyagraha, promoted nationally by the Congress, started creating cracks within the organization in which the Gandhians were highly enthused while the other group, the Swarajists, called it inconsequential.

Finally, at the All India Congress Committee meeting in July 1923, at the insistence of Jawaharlal Nehru and Sarojini Naidu, Congress closed ranks and the flag movement was endorsed.

The flag movement was managed by Sardar Vallabhbhai Patel with the idea of public processions and flag displays by common people. By the end of the movement, over 1500 people had been arrested across all of British India.

The Bombay Chronicle reported that the movement drew from diverse groups of society, including farmers, students, merchants, laborers, and "national servants." While Muslim participation was moderate, the movement enthused women, who had hitherto rarely participated in the independence movement.

While the flag agitation got its impetus from Gandhi's writings and discourses, the movement received political acceptance following the Nagpur incident.

News reports, editorials, and letters to editors published in various journals and newspapers of the time attest to the subsequent development of a bond between the flag and the nation.

Soon, the concept of preserving the honor of the national flag became an integral component of the independence struggle. While Muslims were still wary of the Swaraj flag, it gained acceptance among Muslim leaders of the Congress and the Khilafat Movement as the national flag.

The Congress met in Lahore under the presidency of Jawaharlal Nehru in 1929.

It declared Poorna Swaraj or complete independence for India, as its goal. At midnight on December 31, 1929, the tricolor flag was unfurled on the bank of the river Ravi amidst the Slogans Vande Mataram by Jawahar Lal Nehru.

Flag hoisted at Lahore Congress Session

The Indian National Congress appointed a seven-member Flag Committee in 1931 to design a new flag for India:

The committee was appointed at the Congress Working Committee meeting in Karachi on April 2, 1931.

The committee invited opinions from various organizations, provincial Congress Committees, and individuals. They then recommended a flag with an all-saffron color and a brown Charkha in the canton, but it was not accepted.

The Congress Committee met in Karachi in 1931, and adopted the tricolor flag designed by Pingali Venkaiah. The flag had three horizontal stripes of saffron, white, and green, with a charkha in the middle.

The flag was adopted as the official flag of the Congress party in the 1931 Karachi session under the presidency of Sardar Vallabh Bhai Patel. The colour red was changed to saffron on the request of the Sikhs and also it was like the flag of Bulgaria. The flag was modified accordingly.

Since 1921, Venkaiah's flag has been used formally at all Congress meetings.

The flag of Bulgaria

Detractors of the flag movement, including Motilal Nehru, soon hailed the *Swaraj* flag as a symbol of national unity. Thus, the flag became a significant structural component of the institution of India.

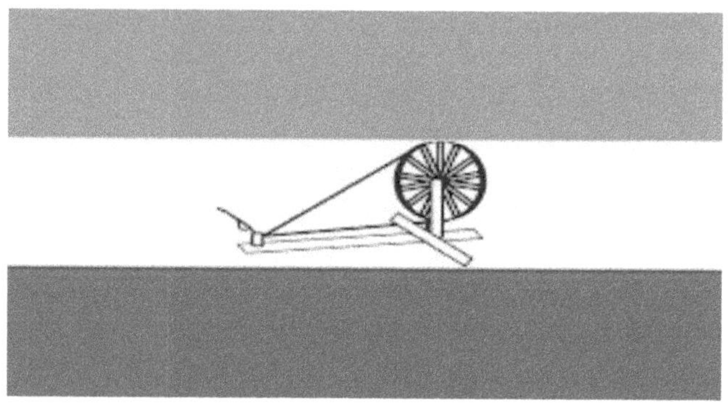

In contrast to the subdued responses of the past, the British Indian government took greater cognizance of the new flag and began to define a policy of response.

The British parliament discussed public use of the flag, and based on directives from London, the British Indian government threatened to withdraw funds from municipalities and local governments that did not prevent the display of the Swaraj flag.

The Swaraj flag became the official flag of Congress at the 1931 meeting. However, by then, the flag had already become the symbol of the independence movement.

Indian National Symbols
National Flag, Emblem & Anthem

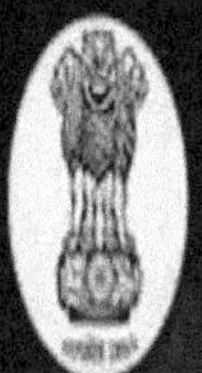

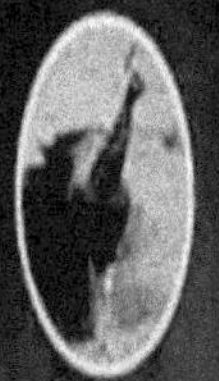

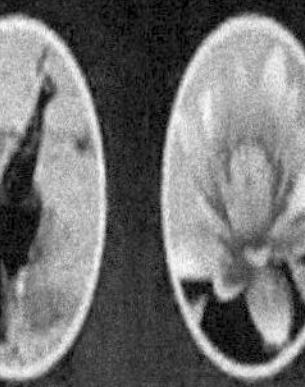

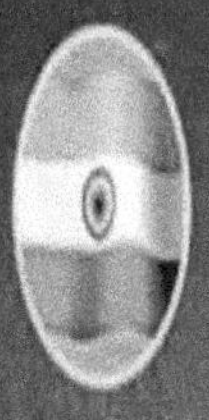

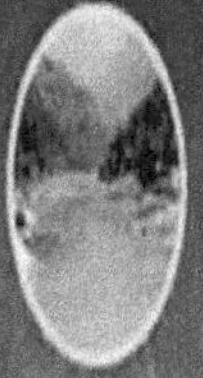

Chapter FOUR

The Flag Resolution 1947

The first President of the independent India was Babu Rajendra Prasad. In his chairmanship, a flag committee of twelve members was formed to make resolutions and for adopting the national flag of India on June 23, 1947.

The members of the flag committee are:

1. Abdul Kalam Azad

2. Rajagopalachari

3. Sarojini Naidu

4. KM. Panikkar

5. KM. Munshi

6. BR. Ambedkar

7. Frank Antony

8. B. Pattabhi Sitaramayya

9. Hiralal Shastri

10. Satyanarayana Siha

11. Baldev Singh

12. SN. Gupta

Photo is not available.

Since the president felt that there was a strong feeling in the country in favor of adopting the national flag adopted by the Congress in 1931 as the national flag, the resolutions passed in the Congress committees were circulated to the members of the ad hoc committee.

Further, the committee considered a note by SD Kalelkar of Nagapur, and the final decision on the design of the flag was taken on July 18.

Originally, the flag had three horizontal strips of white, green and red in the order, starting from the top, with the figure of Charkha superimposed. At a later stage, the red strip was replaced by the orange (to recognize the sacrifices of the saffron-clad Desh-sevikas, as some thought) and the order was changed to orange, white and green, with the charkha in the centre.

On July 22, 1947, a resolution was moved by Jawahar Lal Nehru, who accepted the flag adopted in the Congress committee in 1931 as the national flag.

The flag designed by Pingali Venkaiah in 1921, with the guidance of Gandhiji and Lala Hansraj featuring a spinning wheel at the center, which was ultimately selected by the committee.

The charkha was not symmetrical. It looks different on each side. The committee decided to replace charkha with Ashok chakra of Sarnath. It has 24 spokes and looks the same on both sides.

The decision was made to ensure a more uniform and visually appealing design for the national emblem. The Ashok Chakra is a symbol of progress and righteousness, embodying the values of the nation. Gandhiji was also convinced with this idea, half heartily.

This design was later modified slightly to include the navy-blue color and was officially adopted as the national flag of India on July 22, 1947.

Pandit Jawahar Lal Nehru categorically informed the constituent assembly in his speech on adopting the tricolor as the national flag that the same flag that was used in the struggle for freedom is slightly modified and accepted.

The Ashok Chakra represents the eternal wheel of law and is a powerful symbol of India's rich heritage. Its incorporation into the national emblem was seen as a fitting tribute to the country's history and values.

Gandhiji's approval and Nehru's endorsement further solidified its significance in representing India's journey towards independence and progress.

The following screenshots are from the resolution that adopted the Congress flag as the national flag with some modifications. They are self-explanatory.

concentrated history through which all of us have passed during the last quarter of a century. Memories crowd upon me. I remember the ups and downs of the great struggle for freedom of this great nation. I remember and many in this House will remember how we looked up to this Flag not only with pride and enthusiasm but with a tingling in our veins; also how; when we were sometimes down and out, then again the sight of this Flag gave us courage to go on. Then, many who are not present here today, many of our comrades who have passed, held on to this Flag, some amongst them even unto death. and handed it over as they sank, to others to hold it aloft. So, in this simple form of words, there is much more than will be clear on the surface. There is the struggle of the people for freedom with all its ups and downs and trials and disasters and there is, finally today as I move this Resolution, a certain triumph about it a measure of triumph in the conclusion of that struggle.

Seth Govind Das (C. P. and Berar: General): *[Mr. President, I have come here to support the resolution moved by Pandit Jawaharlal Nehru. I consider this day a landmark in the history of India. Today, Independent India is displaying her national flag. Everyone who, has taken part in the struggle for freedom during the last twenty-seven years is today reminded like Panditji of the events during that period. We were unarmed and helpless and had no resources for achieving independence. But the way in which this battle of freedom has been fought and victory achieved has no parallel, not only in the history of India but also in the history of the world. Today we are achieving the victory for which we were trying for the last so many years. We are also reminded of those who came forward so many times to, pull down this flag, to trample it and to set fire to it. But when Truth and Justice were with us, it was altogether impossible to trample it and to finish it in that way. After twenty-seven years we have been able to prove to the world that even an unarmed nation with no resources at its command, can achieve freedom, if it follows the path of Justice and Truth.

Today. I am reminded of the day when in 1922, Pandit Motilal Nehru came to Jubbulpore for the first time. I am a resident of Jubbulpore. That was the first time when this flag was displayed in India. At that time it had three colours-red, white and green. It was a tricolour no doubt. At that time, this flag was hoisted over the Town Hall of Jubbulpore for the first time in India. Who is not reminded of Pandit Motilal on seeing Pandit Jawaharlal Nehru? At that time a question was raised in the House of Commons as to how this flag was hoisted over a public hall and the Prime Minister of Great Britain assured the house that no event of the sort would be repeated in India in future. But I am pleased to find today that the flag which was hoisted for the first time twenty-five years ago in Jubbulpore, my home town, will now be unfurled over every public building there. It will be a matter of pride for everyone in India.

On the first hour of August 15, 1947, a delegation of 74 women from all over India, under the leadership of Hansa Mehta, presented the national flag to the chairman of the committee, Babu Rajendra Prasad and the first prime minister of India Pandit Jawahar Lal Nehru.

It could be possible that Suraya Tyabji was included in the delegates due to her help in replacing the charkha with the Ashok chakra or due to the influence of her husband in the PMO.

Please make a note that the Hyderabad state ruled by the Nizam was not part of the nation at that time.

VANDE MATARAM

Vande Mataram !
Sujalam, Suphalam,Malayaja Shitalam,
Shasya shyamalam, Mataram !

Shubhra jyotsna Pulakita yaminim
Phulla Kusumita
Drumadala Shobhinim,
Suhasinim, Sumadhura Bhashinim,
Sukhadam, Varadam, Mataram !

Sapta Kotikantha Kalakala Ninada Karale
Dvisapt Koti Bhujair Dhrita Khara Karavale
Abala Kena Ma Eta Bale !
Bahubala Dharinim,Namami Tarinim,
Ripudalavarinim Mataram !

Tvam Hi Durga
Dashpraharana Dharini.

Kamala, Kamaladalaviharini, Vani,
Vidyadayani, Namami Tvam,
Namami Kamalam,
Amalam, Atulam,
Sujalam, Suphalam, Mataram,
Vande Mataram !

Shyamalam, Saralam,
Susmitam, Bhushitam,
Dharanim, Bharanim Mataram !

CHAPTER FIVE

THE ORIGINS OF THE FLAG

The origins of the flags date back to the prehistoric period. It could have originated probably in India, as the epics of Hindu culture do mention the flags. It is mentioned in the Ramayana, Mahabharata, etc.

Flags were used as symbols of identity, authority, and communication in ancient civilizations.

The practice of using flags eventually spread to other cultures and regions around the world.

Flag used by Sri Ram. Photos: Quora

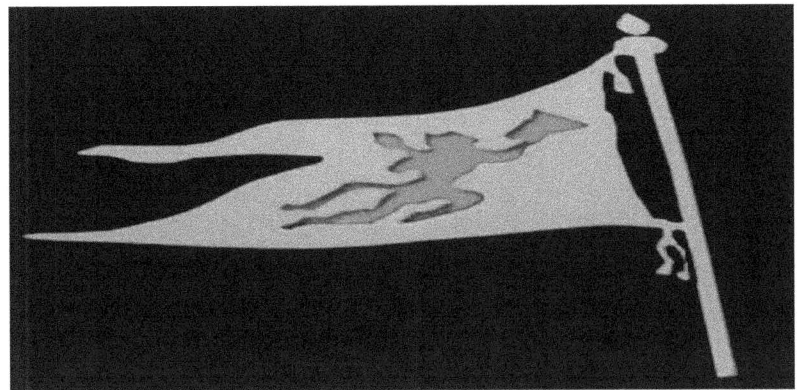

Flag used in Mahabharata by Arjuna Photo: Quora

Flags had equal importance in ancient India, being carried on chariots and elephants. The flag was the first object of attack in battle, and its fall would mean confusion if not defeat. Indian flags were often triangular in shape and scarlet or green in color, with a figure embroidered in gold and a gold fringe.

Flags seem to have been used, in India and China, for signaling, and there is an instance of a white flag being used as a signal for a truce as early as 1542 CE. Indian and Chinese usage spread to Burma (now Myanmar), Siam (now Thailand), and other parts of Southeastern Asia.

The Saracens (a member of any nomadic tribes on the Syrian borders of the Roman Empire. (in later use) an Arab, a Muslim especially in the period of crusades likely transmitted flags to Europe, and the prohibition against using identifiable images as idolatry in Islam shaped their design.

They are often mentioned in the early history of Islam and may have been copied from India, but Islamic flags are greatly simplified and appear to have been plain black, white, or red.

Black was supposed to have been the color of the Prophet Muhammad's banner, the color of vengeance. The ABBASIDS used a black flag in the year 746 CE (AH 129). The Umayyad's contrastingly chose white flags, while the Kharijites used red ones.

Green was the color of the Fatimid dynasty and eventually became the color of Islam. In adopting the crescent sign, however, about 1250, the Ottoman Turks apparently were reverting to an Assyrian sacred symbol of the 9th century BCE and probably of greater antiquity than that. The crescent moon, with or without an additional star or stars, has since become the accepted official symbol of Islam.

In Europe, the first "national" flags were adopted in the Middle Ages and the Renaissance. Many of the leaders of that time adopted the flag of their patron saint to represent their country. In England, for example, the Cross of St. George was adopted in the 13th century.

Toward the end of the Middle Ages, flags had become accepted symbols of countries, kings, organizations, cities, and guilds. Guild flags bore obvious devices. For example, a black flag with three white candles represented the candle makers of Bayeux, France.

The colors and designs of national flags usually are not arbitrarily selected but rather stem from the history, culture, or religion of the particular country. Many flags can be traced to a common origin, and such "flag families" are often linked both by common traditions and by geography.

Nehru to Modi 1947-2024

Every Indian should now forget that
he is a Rajput, a Sikh, or a Jat.
He must remember that he is an Indian.
SARDAR VALLABHBHAI PATEL
Getty/indianexpress.com

CHAPTER SIX

THE FLAGS OF OTHER NATIONS

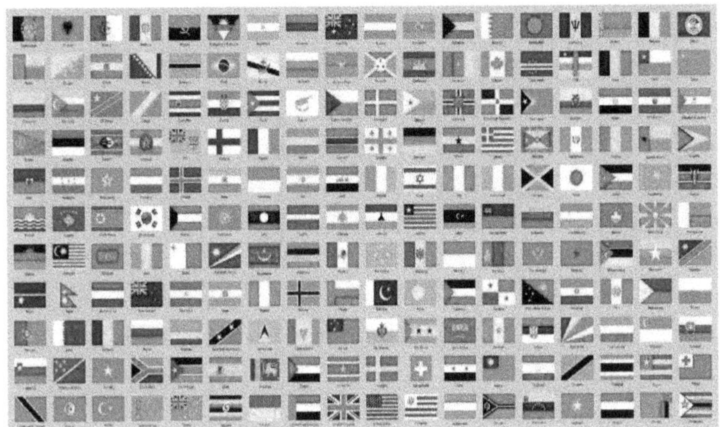

Photo: Vecteezy

There are around 193 nations on the globe, excluding Palestine and the Vatican, which are not UN members. Every country has its own distinct traditions, language, and culture. What makes our earth so lovely and fascinating is the diversity of nations on it.

The nation's pride, the national flag, symbolizes the history and ideals that the nation upholds.

Here are a few national flags from around the world and the designers behind them:

The Flag of the United Kingdom:

King James VI of Scotland and I of England designed the Union Flag, also known as the British flag, in 1606.

The Union Jack or the Union Flag was adopted on January 1, 1801

There was a union of the Scottish and English crowns on 24 March 1603 when James VI of Scotland became the King of England and Ireland as James I.

In 1606 King James proclaimed that there would be one flag that would represent the whole of the United Kingdom, and it was created using the Saltire of Scotland and the St. Georges cross. This was known as the Flag of the Kingdom of Great Britain.

In 1800 the Act of Union enabled the kingdoms of Great Britain and Ireland to join together, and in 1801 the cross of St. Patricks' was added to the flag of the Kingdom of Great

Britain to create the flag of the United Kingdom—the Union Jack (flag), which is in use today.

The Flag of the United States of America USA:

The origin of the first American flag is unknown, but some historians believe that Francis Hopkinson, a New Jersey Congressman and signer of the Declaration of Independence, designed it in 1777.

Hopkinson was the chairman of the Continental Navy Board's Middle Department at the time and was also a naval flag designer. The only evidence of Hopkinson's involvement is a bill he submitted to Congress that mentions designing the flag.

Bob G. Heft is credited with designing the current 50-star American flag. Heft was a high school student who also designed a 51-star flag in case Washington, D.C. or Puerto Rico became a state.

Since its origin in 1777, the American flag has been revised over twenty-four times, and the current one, designed by Heft in 1959, is the twenty-seventh official flag of the United States. The original flag featured 13 stripes along with 13 stars. The current flag still features 13 stripes, but it now has 50 stars.

Heft designed the flag for a school project. The project was to design a new version of the American flag.

For his project, Heft chose to arrange the fifty white stars on a blue background in alternating horizontal rows. Five rows had six stars, and four rows had five stars. Seven alternating horizontal red and six white stripes completed the flag, representing the original thirteen colonies. The flag's three colors, red, white, and blue, represented courage, purity, and justice, respectively. It took Heft 12.5 hours to sew the flag together.

But even after so much hard work, Heft didn't score a perfect grade in this project. His teacher gave him a B, and Heft was left disappointed.

So, he went ahead and discussed his score with the teacher, who jokingly said that if the US Congress selected his design, his grade would be changed to an A.

Heft submitted his design to Congress, and to the surprise of both, Congress chose Heft's design. Heft's grade was changed later to an A. Not only this, shortly after submitting his design to Congress, it was selected as the new American flag.

The Flag of Germany:

The Holy Roman Empire (800/962–1806) known as the Holy Roman Empire of the German Nation after 1512 did not have a national flag, but black and gold were used as colors of the Holy Roman Emperor and featured in the imperial banner: a black eagle in a golden background. After the late 13th or early 14th century, the claws and beak of the eagle were colored red. From the early 15th century, a double-headed eagle was used.

In 1804, Napoleon Bonaparte declared the First French Empire. In response to this, Holy Roman Emperor Francis II of the Habsburg dynasty declared his personal domain to be the Austrian Empire and became Francis I of Austria. Taking the colors of the banner of the Holy Roman Emperor, the flag of the Austrian Empire was black and gold. Francis II was the last Holy Roman Emperor, with Napoleon forcing the empire's dissolution in 1806. After this point, these colors continued to be used as the flag of Austria until 1918.

With the end of the Holy Roman Empire in 1806, many of its dukes and princes joined the Confederation of the Rhine, a confederation of Napoleonic client states. These states preferred to use their own flags. The confederation had no flag of its own; instead, it used the blue-white-red flag of France and the Imperial Standard of its protector, Napoleon.

The 1815–16 Congress of Vienna led to the creation of the German Confederation, a loose union of all remaining German states after the Napoleonic Wars. The Confederation was created as a replacement for the now-extinct Holy Roman Empire, with Francis I of Austria the last Holy Roman Emperor—as its president. The confederation did not have a flag of its own, although the black-red-gold tricolor is sometimes mistakenly attributed to it.

Since the students who served in the Lützow Free Corps came from various German states, the idea of a unified German state began to gain momentum within the Urburschenschaft and similar burschenschafts that were subsequently formed throughout the Confederation.

On 18 October 1817, the fourth anniversary of the Battle of Leipzig, hundreds of fraternity members and academics from across the Confederation states met in Wartburg in Saxe-Weimar-Eisenach (in modern Thuringia), calling for a free and unified German nation.

The gold-red-black flag of the Jena *Urburschenschaft* featured prominently at this Wartburg festival. Therefore, the colors black, red, and gold eventually became symbolic of this desire for a unified German state. The Ministerial Council of the German Confederation, in its determination to maintain the status quo, enacted the Carlsbad Decrees of 1819 that banned all student organizations, officially putting an end to the Burschenschaften.

In May 1832, around 30,000 people demonstrated at the Ham Bach Festival for freedom, unity, and civil rights. The colors black, red, and gold had become a well-established symbol for the liberal, democratic, and republican movement within the German states since the Wartburg Festival, and flags in these colors were flown en masse at the Ham Bach Festival.

On 24 February 1924, the organization Reich banner Schwarz-Rot-Gold was founded in Magdeburg by the member parties of the Weimar Coalition (Centre, DDP, SPD) and the trade unions.

This organization was formed to protect the fragile democracy of the Weimar Republic, which was under constant pressure by both the far right and far left. Through this organization, the black-red-gold flag became not only a symbol of German democracy but also of resistance to political extremism. Otto Horsing, the organization's first chairman, described their task as a struggle against the swastika and the "Soviet star."

In the face of the increasingly violent conflicts between the communists and Nazis, the growing polarization of the

German population, and a multitude of other factors, mainly the drastic economic sinking, extreme hyperinflation, and corruption of the republic, the Weimar Republic collapsed in 1933 with the Nazi seizure of power (Machtergreifung) and the appointment of Adolf Hitler as German Chancellor.

After World War II, Germany was divided into two nations, West Germany and East Germany, until 1989.

After the fall of the Berlin Wall in November 1989, many East Germans removed the coat of arms from their flags to imply the plain black-red-gold tricolor symbol of a united Germany.

Finally, on 3 October 1990, as the area of the German Democratic Republic was absorbed into the Federal Republic of Germany, the black-red-gold tricolor became the flag of a reunified Germany.

Flag of Germany under the NAZI rule

The flag of France:

The French flag, also known as the tricolor (three-color) flag, **has its origins in the French Revolution of 1789.** The French people chose the three colors, blue, white, and red, to represent their important values: blue for freedom, white for equality, and red for fraternity, in the flag.

- **White**

  The color of the king, which represented loyalty to the country and unwavering devotion. During the revolution, white also took on a new meaning as a symbol of protection.

- **Blue and red**

The colors of Paris, which were used on the city's coat of arms and later became the royal coat of arms. The combination of these colors symbolized the alliance between the king and the people.

The original flag design had red first, then white, then blue, but the order was changed in 1794. After Napoleon was defeated in 1815, the flag was changed to a solid white, but King Louis Philippe restored the tricolor in 1830. The flag has been the sole national flag of France since March 5, 1848, and today it flies over all public buildings.

The Russian Flag:

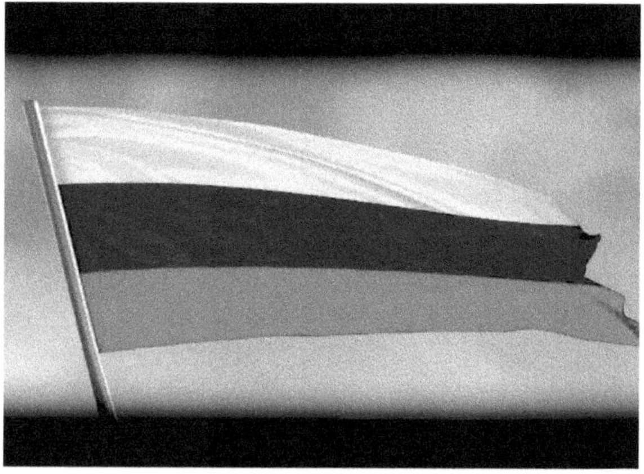

Tsar Peter I the Great had ambitious plans to transform Russia into a modern state. Building a Russian navy was part of that program, and he visited the Netherlands to learn about the most advanced shipbuilding concepts and techniques.

The flag he chose for merchant ships in 1699 reflected the Dutch red-white-blue tricolor; the Russian flag differed only in having the stripes arranged white-blue-red. These colors are sometimes given traditional Russian symbolism—one such interpretation recalls the red shield of the Grand Principality of Moscow, with its representation of St. George cloaked in blue and mounted on a white horse.

The new flag became very popular, so much so that during the 19th century the black-orange-white tricolor that the tsars attempted to impose as a national flag on land completely failed and eventually was abandoned. Just after the beginning of World War I, the Russian ruling dynasty added a golden yellow canton bearing the imperial arms to the flag as a symbol of solidarity between the dynasty and the Russian people.

In the Soviet era, all Russian flags were based on the Red Banner, which had its roots in the French Revolution and, possibly, even earlier peasant uprisings. After the formation of the Soviet Union, the official state flag contained a gold hammer, sickle, and gold-bordered red star in the upper hoist corner.

When the Soviet Union dissolved, its symbols were replaced. The non-Russian territories acquired by tsars and communist leaders became independent, and the Russian Federation that remained readopted the white-blue-red Russian national flag.

It became official on August 21, 1991, four months before the formal dissolution of the Soviet Union. It is now widely accepted, although a few groups favor the use of the Red Banner or even adoption of the black-orange-white tricolor.

The Flag of China:

The current flag of China, also known as the Five Star Red Flag, was **first raised on October 1, 1949, to mark the establishment of the People's Republic of China**. The flag's design and symbolism have changed over time.

- **Design**

  The flag was designed by Zeng Lian song, an economist from Shanghai who won a competition.

- **Soviet era**

  The flag had a red background with a globe in the center, containing a sickle, hammer, and golden star.

- **After 1949**

   The flag was changed to a crimson field with five golden stars in the canton. The five stars and their relationship to each other have different meanings:

Large star: represents the Communist Party of China (CCP).

Smaller stars: Represent four social classes that the CCP wants to unite: everyday workers, farmers, small business owners, and large industry owners.

Colors

The red background represents communism, the Han people, and good fortune. It also expresses the revolutionary communist philosophy that has been in power since 1949 and is the traditional ethnic color of the Han people.

The flag is displayed in government buildings, schools, airports, train stations, and military organizations.

It is also common to hold flag-raising ceremonies that include the national anthem, and desecrating the flag can result in jail time.

The Japan flag:

Japan's national flag, the Hinomaru, or "sun circle," has been used in various forms since at least 701AD, when **Emperor Monmu** used a sun-motif flag in court ceremonies.

The flag's red circle and circular shape are associated with Amaterasu, the sun goddess and mythical ancestor of the Japanese Imperial family.

The Meiji government officially adopted the Hinomaru as the national flag in 1870 to represent a modernizing and unified Japan, but it wasn't officially adopted until 1999.

Flags of neighboring nations of India:

Pakistan:

Syed Amir-uddin Kedwai and his team created the design that was approved as the national flag. It was officially adopted by the Constituent Assembly of Pakistan on August 11, 1947, a few days before Pakistan gained its independence from British rule.

Upon independence, it became the flag of, first, the Dominion of Pakistan and then, from 23 March 1956, that of the Islamic Republic of Pakistan. The design remains unchanged since its initial adoption.

Bangladesh:

Shib Narayan Das (1946-2024) designed the first version of Bangladesh's national flag, which was based on a flag used during the 1971 Bangladesh Liberation War. Das was a Bangladeshi designer who died in Dhaka on April 19, 2024, at the age of 77. His design inspired the country's current flag, which was formally adopted on January 17, 1972.

A green banner bears a red disc with a golden outline of Bangladesh, symbolizing the natural beauty of the country and the bloodshed of Bengalis in their struggle for independence. The disc represents the rising sun of a new country.

Shankar Nath Rimal, a Nepalese architect and civil engineer, standardized the current Nepalese flag in 1962 at the request of King Mahendra. Two rival branches of the ruling dynasty previously used pennants that were later combined to create the flag, based on the original design used in the 19th and 20th centuries.

The flag was officially adopted on December 16, 1962, along with the formation of a new constitutional government.

Bhutan:

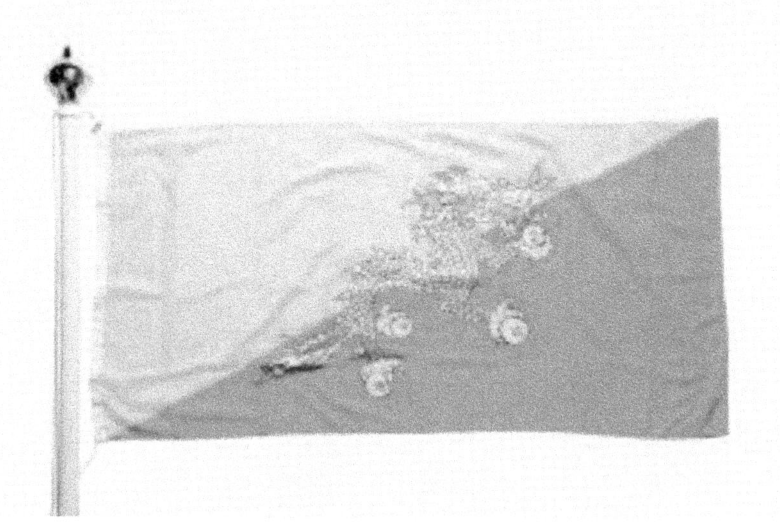

Mayum Choying Wangmo Dorji designed the Bhutanese flag in 1947. The flag is based on the Drukpa Lineage of Tibetan Buddhism, which is the main religion in Bhutan. The flag has undergone several changes since its design, including changes to the colors and dimensions:

- **1949**

  The flag was first displayed during negotiations between Bhutan and India, and it was similar to the current flag but with a pale green dragon.

- **1956**

  A second version was introduced for the visit of Druk Gyalpo Jigme Dorji Wangchuk to eastern Bhutan, and it featured a white dragon instead of the green one.

- **1969**

  King Jigme Dorji Wangchuck requested more changes to the flag, including making it a rectangle, changing the red to orange, and relaxing the dragon's body. The flag has remained the same since then, except for the introduction of a code of conduct in 1972 that specifies the flag's size and how it should be flown.

The flag's colors and symbols have specific meanings:

- Yellow: represents the heritage and power of the Dragon King, the leader of Bhutan.

- Orange: symbolizes Buddhism, similar to the robes worn by Buddhist monks of the Drukpa tradition.

- White: Represents the purity of the dragon

- Jewels: Represent Bhutan's wealth and security

The flag is unique because it is one of the few national flags to feature an animal, in this case a dragon known as Druk, which is a central part of Bhutanese culture and history. Bhutan is also known as the Land of the Thunder Dragon because Bhutanese mythology says that the sound of thunder is the voice of dragons, and Druk is the dragon of thunder.

Sri Lanka:

A committee appointed by **D.S. Senanayake**, the first Prime Minister of independent Sri Lanka, designed the Sri Lankan flag. The committee approved the design in February 1950, and the flag was first raised on March 3, 1950. The flag incorporates symbols from the civil standard of the last king of Sri Lanka, as well as other elements:

- Lion: A passant royal lion with a sword in its right forepaw

- Bo-leaves: Four bow-leaves, one in each corner, that represent Buddhism and its influence on the country

- Stripes: Two vertical stripes, green and orange, that represent the minority Muslim and Tamil races, respectively.

- Border: represents other minor races

The flag also represents the four virtues of kindness, friendliness, happiness, and equanimity.

Photo courtesy: Times of India

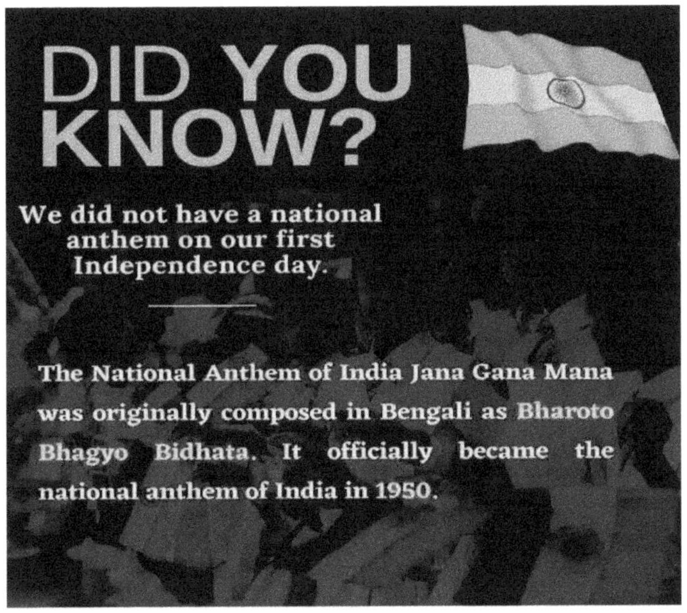

CHAPTER SEVEN

THE TYABJI FAMILY

Badruddin Tyabji:

Tyabji was born on 10 October 1844 in Bombay (Mumbai), part of the Bombay Presidency of British India. He was the son of Mullah Tyab Ali Bhai Mian, a member of the Sulamani Bohra community and a scion of an old Cambay emigrant Arab family.

He studied law in London and the Middle Temple between 1863 and 1867. In between, he came to India due to health reasons. On his return to Bombay in December 1867, Tyabji became the first Indian barrister in the High Court of Bombay.

Badruddin and his elder brother Camruddin were deeply involved in the founding of the Indian National Congress. Tyabji was instrumental in building the national scope of the Congress by working to gain support from both Hindus and Muslims, and during his time as President of the Indian National Congress between 1887 and 1888, he focused on uniting the Muslim community.

To promote social interaction among the city's Muslims, Tyabji was instrumental in founding both the Islam Club and the Islam Gymkhana. He was one of the founding members of the Congress.

In June 1895, Tyabji was made a judge of the Bombay High Court, the first Muslim and the third Indian to be so elevated. In 1902, he became the first Indian to hold the post of Chief Justice of the Bombay High Court.

On 26 August 1906, while on a furlough in London, England, Badruddin Tyabji died suddenly of a heart attack.

Badruddin Faiz Tyabji (1907–1995) was a senior Indian Civil Service officer who served as vice chancellor of the Aligarh Muslim University from 1962 to 1965. **He is the grandson of Badruddin Tyabji.**

He was born in Bombay. His father was Faiz Tyabji, a judge of the Bombay High Court. His sister Kamila Tyabji was a lawyer and philanthropist. While serving as a diplomat in 1948, he had undertaken the task of starting the Embassy of India, Brussels. He also served as Indian ambassador in Jakarta, Tehran, Bonn, and Tokyo.

Surayya Tyabji (1919–1978) was an Indian artist who assisted in creating the current Indian national flag by adding the Ashoka Chakra from the Lion Capital of Ashoka (Saranath), replacing the Charkha on the 1931 flag of the Indian National Congress.

The family of Badruddin Faiz Tyabji

She was the niece of Sir Akbar Hydari, who served as the Prime Minister of Hyderabad from 1937 to 1941. She was married to Badruddin Faiz Tyabji, a civil servant of Bombay.

CONCLUSION

Who designed the Indian national flag? The answer is simple. It depends upon the reader's mindset. It is Pingali Venkaiah, not Suraya Tyabji, who is the architect of the flag, according to all available records.

She helped the flag committee to replace the charkha and imposed the Ashok Chakra as recommended. She got that opportunity as she was the wife of an ICS officer in PMO and an artist.

It is not fair to disregard the efforts of a freedom fighter and the person who conceptualized the need for a flag. Pingali Venkaiah, a freedom fighter and multi-talented person, is credited with designing the Indian national flag.

Suraya Tyabji's role in the flag committee was significant, but it was Venkaiah who ultimately created the final design that we see today.

Bapu Museum Vijayawada

ABOUT THE AUTHOR

The author is the third son of a bank employee, Late GV Narasimham, and a housewife, Seetha Maha Lakshmi, who is the only daughter of Pingali Venkaiah, architect of the Indian national flag.

The author started his career as an associate editor of a Telugu political magazine and worked for six years until 1984. Later, he went to the UAE and worked in various positions in marketing and construction domains for ten years. He returned to India in 1994 to continue in marketing and skill training until 2019 in a senior position. He took his retirement.

Through his extensive research and personal insights obtained from his mother, who recently died, and the only daughter of Pingali Venkaiah, and his elder brother, who saw his grandfather personally. The author hopes to bring awareness to the true origins of the Indian flag and its designer.

The author's book sheds light on the importance of recognizing Pingali Venkaiah's contribution to India's national flag and aims to educate readers on the history and significance of this iconic symbol.

Author contact details:

Ghantasala Gopi Krishna

Flat No# 506, Sai Suvarna Enclave

Sainathapuram

AS Rao Nagar

Hyderabad-500062

Mobile:9885624099

e-mail: ghantasalagopikrishna@gmail.com

www.ingramcontent.com/pod-product-compliance
Lightning Source LLC
Chambersburg PA
CBHW040127150726
48005CB00015B/2400